MY ADVENTURES IN NURSERY RHYME LAND

This book was especially
written for
Jacob Threadgould
with love and kisses
from
Auntie Jennifer

Written & Illustrated
by
Margaret Gibson

Little Bo-Peep has lost her sheep,
And doesn't know where to find them.

Poor little Bo-Peep!
She asked Mother Goose if she
knew where to find the sheep.

Mother Goose had a house,
'Twas built in a wood,
Where an owl at the door
For sentinel stood.

Mother Goose knew just the person who could help her find Little Bo-Peep's sheep.

Old Mother Goose
When she wanted to wander
Would ride through the air
On a very fine gander.

She flew to 16 Ferrygate, North Berwick.

'Hello, Jacob,' she said. 'I'm looking for Little Bo-Peep's sheep and you're just the person who can help me.'

'Can his friends come too?' asked Jacob. Mother Goose smiled.

'Only a child born on the tenth of August can be my special helper.'

'Climb up onto the back of my gander and hold on very tightly,' she said. 'Off we go to Nursery Rhyme Land.'

Jacob held on tightly as they flew away across the sea towards Nursery Rhyme Land.

'Look down below,' cried Jacob. 'There are three funny men floating on the water in a tub.'

Rub-a-dub-dub,
Three men in a tub,
And how do you think they got there?
The butcher, the baker,
The candlestick maker,
They all jumped out of a rotten potato,
'Twas enough to make us all stare.

'Have you seen Little Bo-Peep's sheep?' called Jacob.

'Not I,' replied the butcher.

'Not I,' replied the baker.

'Not I,' replied the candlestick maker.

'Fly on, Mother Goose,' said Jacob. 'The three men in a tub can't help us.'

'Look, on that big hill up ahead!' cried Mother Goose. 'We'll ask those two children if they have seen the sheep.'
The gander and its two passengers landed on the steep grassy hill.

'Why, it's Jack and Jill,' said Jacob. 'Have you seen Little Bo-Peep's sheep?'

'Not I,' said Jack.

'Not I,' said Jill. 'We're too busy fetching some water.'

Jack and Jill
Went up the hill
To fetch a pail of water;
Jack fell down
And broke his crown,
And Jill came tumbling after.

'I hope Jack and Jill will be all right,' said Jacob.

'I'm sure they will be,' replied Mother Goose. 'Let's find someone else to help us.'

'Look!' called Jacob. 'There is a little girl running across the grass. Maybe she has seen Little Bo-Peep's sheep.'

Little Miss Muffet
Sat on a tuffet,
Eating her curds and whey:
There came a big spider
Who sat down beside her
And frightened Miss Muffet away.

'Have you seen Little Bo-Peep's sheep?' asked Jacob.

'Not I,' cried Miss Muffet. 'I'm running away from the big spider.'

'I'm not afraid of spiders,' laughed Jacob. 'I think we should find someone else to help us.'

Mother Goose led the way towards a large haystack.

'Ssh,' she whispered.

'That little boy is sound asleep.'

Little Boy Blue
Come blow your horn,
The sheep's in the meadow
The cow's in the corn.
Where is the boy
Who looks after the sheep?
He's under the haystack
Fast asleep.

Will you wake him?
No, not I
For if I do
He's sure to cry.

'He can't help us,' said Jacob.

'And there's only one sheep in the meadow,' said Mother Goose.

Just then they noticed a little girl walking towards them.

'Look, Mother Goose,' cried Jacob. 'She has a lamb with her. She must know where all the sheep have gone.'

Mary had a little lamb,
Its fleece was white as snow;
And everywhere that Mary went
The lamb was sure to go.

It followed her to school one day
That was against the rule;
It made the children laugh and play
To see a lamb at school.

'Excuse me,' said Jacob. 'We're looking for Little Bo-Peep's sheep. Can you help us?'

'Not I,' said Mary. 'My lamb has followed me to school. I must return it to my home and my beautiful garden.' And off she walked.

'Mary, Mary, quite contrary,
How does your garden grow?'

'With silver bells and cockle shells,
And pretty maids all in a row.'

Mother Goose looked very disappointed.
'I thought Mary could have helped us,' she said.
There, ahead of them, stood a strange house
with many children playing.
'Let's ask them if they've seen Little
Bo-Peep's sheep.'

There was an old woman
who lived in a shoe,
She had so many children
she didn't know what to do;
She gave them some broth
without any bread,
And whipped them all soundly
and sent them to bed.

'Too late,' said Jacob. 'It's growing dark and their mother has chased them all inside.' Jacob, Mother Goose and the gander walked past the strange house until they found their way blocked by a large wall.
Looking up Jacob cried,
'Why, it's Humpty Dumpty!'

Humpty Dumpty sat on a wall,
Humpty Dumpty had a great fall;
All the King's horses and all the King's men
Couldn't put Humpty together again.

'Too late,' said Mother Goose. 'He's fallen off!' They walked around the wall and looked at poor Humpty Dumpty.

'I can hear galloping horses,' announced Jacob. 'We'd better leave quickly before the King's men arrive.'

So they climbed onto the gander's back and flew up into the darkening sky.

'Look, look down there!' cried Jacob. 'I can see lots of sheep.'

And there, beneath them, they saw many black and white sheep walking along the lane.

'That's Little Bo-Peep leading her sheep,' smiled Mother Goose. 'I wonder whether she knows they are behind her?'

'I know what happened!' cried Jacob excitedly, and he called down to Little Bo-Peep:

'Look behind you, Little Bo-Peep! You have forgotten the ending of your nursery rhyme:

Little Bo-Peep has lost her sheep
And doesn't know where to find them.
Leave them alone
And they will come home
Bringing their tails behind them.'

'What a clever helper you've been,' said Mother Goose. 'And now I have to return you safely home.'
So the gander flew high in the night sky taking his passengers far away from Nursery Rhyme Land.

Gently they landed outside Jacob's home in North Berwick. Mother Goose carried sleepy Jacob into his bedroom, tucked him into bed and whispered,

'Goodnight, Jacob. Thank you for remembering the end of Little Bo-Peep's nursery rhyme.'

Mother Goose said goodbye
And caught her gander soon,
Climbed on to its broad white back
And flew up to the moon.